CREATED,
ILLUSTRATED
& WRITTEN
BY

SNARES
@SNARESART
(TWITTER)

ART
ASSISTANCE
BY

DONRYU
@DONRYUART
(TWITTER)

THIS BOOK IS
DEDICATED TO
THE FURRY FANDOM

FOR ALL THE
INSPIRATION, KINDNESS, GUIDANCE,
FRIENDSHIPS AND SUPPORT
THE COMMUNITY HAS GIVEN ME,
I HOPE I'VE BEEN ABLE TO REPAY
IT IN SOME CAPACITY OR ANOTHER.

THANK YOU.

FONTS BY
BLAMBOT.COM

MEATIER
SHOWERS

THIS IS WHERE I WORK. SURE, IT LOOKS SHADY AND ALL, BUT DON'T LET THAT GET TO YOU.

MEATIER SHOWERS

OUR CLIENTS PREFER TO BE DISCREET. MOST ONLY KNOW US THROUGH WORD OF MOUTH.

AND IF THAT SIGN ISN'T ENOUGH OF A CLUE...

MEATIER SHOWERS

WELL, NAME'S GROOVER. I'M A SERVICE ASSISTANT AT A LOCAL GAY BATHHOUSE. IT DON'T PAY MUCH, BUT I MANAGE.

HEY!

PLENTY OF ACTION GOES ON HERE EVERY NIGHT, BUT THAT SHOULDN'T COME AS A SURPRISE...

UH! UHNGH! HARDER!!

...IN A BUSINESS LIKE THIS WHERE CUSTOMERS LITERALLY CUM AND GO.

ALSO, THE PLACE *ALWAYS* REEKS OF SEX...

...SOMETHING I'LL NEVER QUITE GET USED TO.

IT'S MY JOB TO MOP IT ALL UP...

AND AT TIMES IT CAN BE RATHER LONELY.

PROBABLY NOT THE BEST PLACE TO FIND THAT "SPECIAL SOMEONE"...

MEATIER SHOWERS GYM

BUT WHEN YOU SEE THE CUDDLING, HAND-HOLDING AND KISSES...

IT GETS TO ME SOMETIMES.

SIGH...

OH...

MY...

MUSCLE GOD OF LOVE!

A RIPPLING STRUCTURE OF SHEER SIZE AND POWER.

EVERY MUSCLE-PUMPING ACTION, EVERY VIGOROUS FLEX HE DOES...

...IS MAKING ME WISH I HAD A SPARE CHANGE OF PANTS RIGHT NOW.

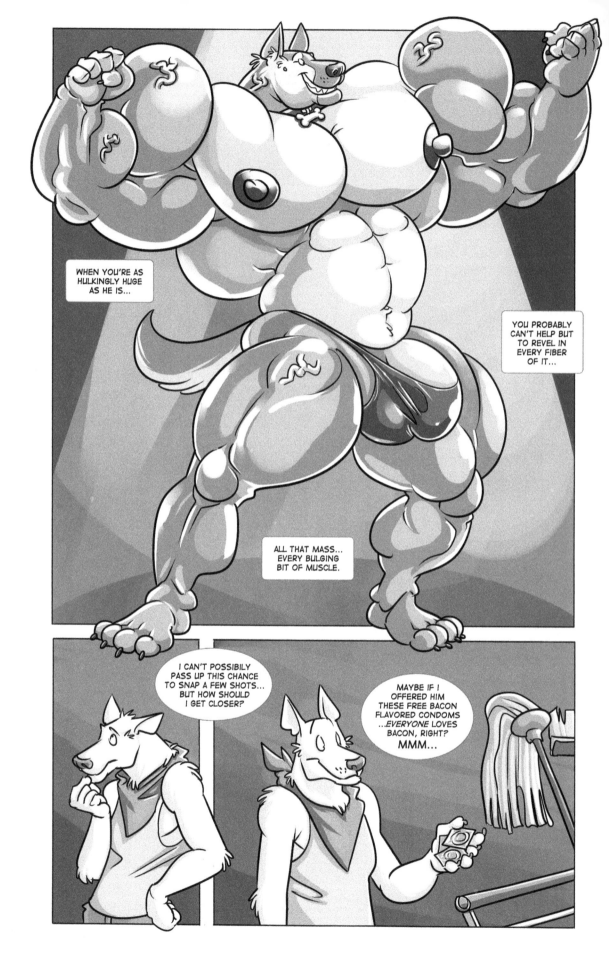

LATER THAT EVENING...

MEATIER SHOWERS

AND REMEMBER TO TURN OFF THE LIGHTS WHEN YOU'RE FINALLY DONE WITH WORK!

GREAT, HE'S GONE... LEAST I CAN TAKE A BREAK NOW, SINCE IT'S ALREADY TIME TO CLOSE...

PANT! GASP!

SLAM!

DAMMIT, I NEVER GOT THE GUY'S NAME OR NUMBER!

SIGH... WHO KNOWS WHEN WE'LL EVER MEET AGAIN...?

I JUST WANNA OGLE AND JIZZ ALL OVER YOU!

SOMETHING TELLS ME I SHOULDN'T STILL BE HERE...

PERHAPS, NOW...

I CAN HAVE A LITTLE FUN OF MY OWN...

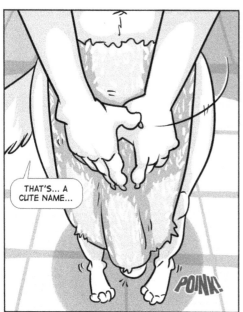

I'M NOT SURE IF I'M DRAWN TOWARDS TANZ FOR WHAT HE IS ON THE *OUTSIDE*... OR WHO HE IS ON THE *INSIDE*...

TRUTH IS, IT COULD BE *BOTH*. BUT HEY, WHAT'S THE RUSH? THERE'S PLENTY OF TIME TO BETTER KNOW EACH OTHER...

...OVER SOME REALLY GOOD COFFEE AND WAFFLES!

AND WHEN I *DO* ARRIVE AT AN ANSWER...

LEAST IT'LL BE THE *TRUTH*.

AS FOR NOW, WE JUST ENJOY EACH OTHER'S COMPANY.

WHAT CAN I SAY? WORK JUST GOT A LOT *MEATIER* THESE DAYS.

SPECIAL DELIVERY!

YOU'RE HERE EARLY!

GOT SOME *HUGE* PACKAGES FOR YA!

YOU REALLY GOTTA STOP SAYING THAT WHEN YOU'RE *THIS* CLOSE.

I HEARD YOU TOOK THE REST OF THE DAY OFF?

YEP, SURE DID!

GONNA BE MEETING SOMEONE SPECIAL TONIGHT!

BITZZ!

MEATIER SHOWERS

YOU FOUND YOURSELF A DATE? THAT'S WONDERFUL! WHAT'S HE LIKE?

STAFF ONLY
NO UNAUTHORIZED ENTRY

BEFORE YOU DECIDE ON TAKING A BREAK, HAVE YOU:

CLEANED THE SHOWERS
REPLACED TOILET PAPERS
MOPPED ALL FLOORS
WIPED ALL SURFACES
RECEIVED MY CONSENT

SIGH...

I JUST CAN'T SEEM TO TAKE MY MIND OFF HIM...

WELL, NOT THAT I'D WANT TO, BUT...

HIS VOICE... THE WAY HE TALKS... EVERYTHING! HE'S JUST SO DREAMY!

GROOVER...

I JUST HAVE TO CALL HIM NOW!

GROOVER?

... BUT THEN HE'S GONNA THINK I'M ALL SO CLINGY AND CREEPY!

GROOVER!!!

GUH!

WELL, LOOKS LIKE THE BOSS ALREADY LEFT...

GUESS THAT MEANS A SHIFT IN MY SCHEDULE!

FIRE ALARM
USE ONLY IN THE EVENT OF AN EMERGENCY

WHAM!!

RIIIIINNGG!!!

OW OW OW.

RIIIIINNNGGGGG

EVERYBODY OUT NOW! SHOWER TIME'S OVER!

THE ROOF IS ON FIRE!!

BUSINESS AS USUAL TOMORROW THOUGH!

GAAAAHHH!!

AND NOW FOR LARGER MATTERS AT HAND...

GGRRRRRRRRRR...

HAH.

YOU *ALMOST* HAD ME THERE.

GETTING ME ALL WORKED UP LIKE THAT? THIS YOUR IDEA OF SOME KIND OF *TEST*?

IT'S FUNNY, CAUSE GROOVER NEVER SAW YOU AS THE CARING SORT...

I DON'T *CARE* ABOUT THAT DUMBASS KID... I PAY HIM – HE'S MY *EMPLOYEE*. I LAY THE GROUND RULES, PERIOD.

BUT YOU *DO*, DON'T YOU?

GET LAID.

LATER THAT EVENING...

I'LL HAVE THE USUAL.

I'LL HAVE THE SAME AS HIM.

PAYS TO BE PREPARED...

POCKET PICK UP LINES Conversation Cards

SO, DO YOU LIKE PLANETS? I'M ALL FOR URANUS...

NO WAIT, SCRAP THAT.

NICE WEATHER OUTSIDE, I LOVE GETTING BLOWN ONCE IN UH...

WHAT?!

FLIP!

FLIP!

J-JUST GIVE ME A MOMENT! I CAN'T SEEM TO FIND THE RIGHT THING TO SAY!

ORDER OF 2 LARGE WAFFLES SMOTHERED IN BLUEBERRY SAUCE...

BLAAH!

!!!

OMPH!

I AM *SO* SORRY ABOUT WHAT HAPPENED!

IT'S ALL GOOD, GROOVER. YOU DON'T HAVE TO KEEP APOLOGIZING!

I JUST WANTED DINNER TO BE PERFECT... I'M SUCH A MESS...

IT'S NO WONDER WHY MY BOSS *HATES* ME...

GROOVER, WE ALL MAKE MISTAKES ONCE IN AWHILE. DON'T BE SO HARD ON YOURSELF! IT'S JUST BLUEBERRY SAUCE, AND BESIDES...

YOUR BOSS DOESN'T REALLY HATE YOU...

HOW WOULD YOU KNOW?

CAUSE DEEP DOWN INSIDE HE CARES...?

RIIITE... THAT'LL BE THE DAY!

C'MON, LET'S GET YOU CLEANED UP!

WILL YOUR BOSS BE BACK TO CHECK ON YOU?

OH, NOT TO WORRY. I'VE HAD ALL THE ENTRANCES BARRICADED WITH FURNITURE.

ANYWAY, YOU CAN TAKE A SHOWER WHILE WAITING FOR YOUR CLOTHES.

THIS HERE'S RESERVED FOR CLUB MEMBERS ONLY.

THE STUDGAZER SUITE.

AND I GET TO USE IT FOR FREE TONIGHT?

SWEET.

ANY REASON WHY IT'S CALLED THE 'STUD-GAZER' SUITE?

'S-STUD-GAZER'? DID I SAY THAT? UH... I MEANT 'STARGAZER', YEAH.

YOU KNOW, 'TARS', NOT... 'STUDS'...

I'LL UH... LEAVE YOU TO YOUR SHOWER NOW! ENJOY!

SLAM!!!

?

GUESS I'LL JUST MAKE MYSELF COMFORTABLE.

HEH, WHAT A MESS.

SHUFFLE SHUFFLE

STRETCH

?

PANT PANT PANT

IT'S COMING FROM...

WELL... I'VE GOT A HUNCH WHY THIS IS CALLED THE 'STUDGAZER' SUITE NOW.

AND PRETTY SURE KNOW WHO'S BEHIND THAT MIRROR...

PANT PANT PANT

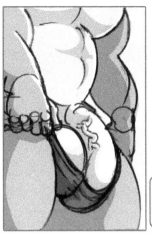

PHWISSHHH

ITS ODD THOUGH, YOU'D THINK THAT BY NOW...

HE'D HAVE STUCK SOMETHING OUT THROUGH THAT HOLE, OR AM I SUPPOSED TO START...?

THE TRUTH IS, I'D BARELY FIT THROUGH EVEN IF I'D WANTED TO.

PSSSSHHHH

WELL, WHATEVER IT IS, I SURE HOPE YOU'RE ENJOYING THE SHOW.

CAN'T TELL IF YOU'RE JUST PLAIN SHY...

PLAYIN' IT SAFE...

OR JUST HAVING SOME FUN OF YOUR OWN NOW...

FWAP!
FWAP!
FWAP!

MOMENTS LATER...

AND HOW WAS YOUR SHOWER?

HE REALLY THINKS I HADN'T NOTICED...

OH! VERY REFRESHING, TO SAY THE LEAST...

SHALL WE MOVE ON WITH THE NIGHT'S ACTIVITIES?

WHAT DO YOU HAVE IN MIND?

BOOZE! YOU CAN'T ENJOY THE NIGHT AFTER WORK, NOT WITHOUT SOME GOOD BEER!

DID HE JUST PULL THAT OUT FROM BEHIND THE COUCH?

YEAH!

GROWLS

HERE'S HOPING EITHER ONE OF US GETS DRUNK!

AND NOW FOR SOME MUSIC!

SEEING THAT WE BOTH SHARE SIMILAR TASTES, SHALL WE...

...D-DANCE??

HEH... SH-SURE.

I DON'T REALLY KNOW HOW, THOUGH...

CHUG! CHUG! CHUG!

JUST LEAVE THAT TO ME!

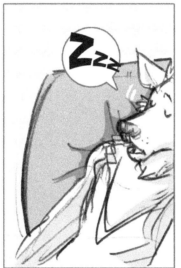

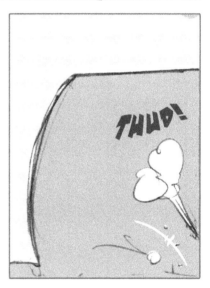

VOL.2
END!

CHAPTER 3

IT'S BEEN AGES SINCE I LAST VISITED A CARNIVAL LIKE THIS...

SAME HERE! I'M GLAD WE DECIDED TO IN THE END...

I'D BE KINDA EMBARRASSED TO BE HERE ON MY OWN...

YEAH, I PROBABLY WOULDN'T THINK OF BEING HERE ALONE EITHER...

THAT'D BE KINDA SAD...

RABID PUPS EVERYWHERE! HAHAHA!

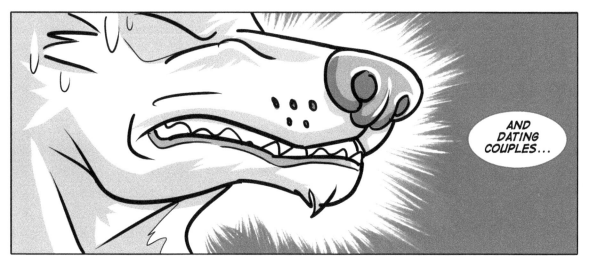

AND DATING COUPLES...

PERHAPS THE FERRIS WHEEL MIGHT'VE BEEN A BETTER CHOICE.

WHAM!

TEST YOUR STRENGTH!

WIELD IT LIKE A MAN!

STEP RIGHT UP!
RING TH
BELL
WIN A PRIZE

GREATEST SHOW ON EARTH!

TICKETS

BEHOLD THE AMAZING HORSE WITH NO NAME

OH MY.

BRANK'S
SUCCULENT
MAN
SAUSAGES
$1.00

WELL, ONLY IF YOU'RE FEELING *COMFORTABLE* WITH THE IDEA, NO PRESSURE THERE–

SURPRISE *KISS!*

SO HERE I AM, WITH THE LOVE OF MY LIFE. AND FOR ONCE, THIS ISN'T ME DREAMING...

HAVING FINALLY BOTH SHOWN OUR HANDS, RETURNING TO THE BATH HOUSE SEEMED LIKE A PLAN...

OUR TESTOSTERONES WERE RAGING AND OUR PRIMAL INSTINCTS HAD TAKEN OVER... WE *HAD* TO DO IT *NOW*.

AWW... *CRAP!* WHAT WERE THE ODDS OF THAT? I LEFT THE DOOR KEYS TO MEATIER SHOWER BACK AT HOME!

I'M SO SORRY. LOOKS LIKE THIS WILL HAVE TO WAIT FOR ANOTHER NIGHT. HOW ABOUT WE HEAD TO A LIBRARY AND SEE IF WE COULD—

ROWR!

GAAAH!

WHAM!

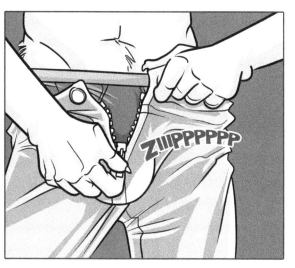

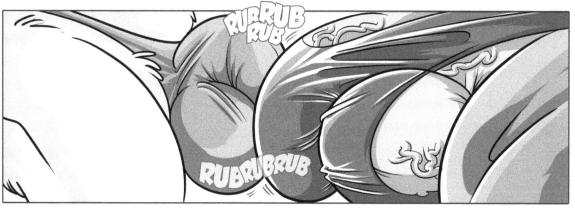

OPEN

CLOSED

HUFF!

SHLURP!

PLAPPLAPPLAP

AROO!

FFHHHPPHTTTBB!!

A FEW DAYS LATER...

MEATIER SHOWERS

WHY, HELLO, MY FRIENDS!!

PREYFORD?

DON'T MIND ME, I'M HERE TO HELP DISTRIBUTE THESE FLYERS FOR OUR COMMUNITY!

ONE NIGHT ONLY

A SPECIAL WEEKEND SHOW AT THE NEARBY BALLROOM!

DO DROP BY IF YOU'RE NOT OCCUPIED THIS EVENING!

OOH! I LIKE HIS HAIR! QUITE THE CUTIE THERE!

NOT SURE IF THE BOSS IS GONNA LET ME...

NOW WHEN WAS THE LAST TIME YOU & I HAD SOME *FUN*, HMM?

NOT SINCE WE MET.

ALWAYS THE CHARMER.

Behind-the-Scenes

Over the course of years since creating the first Meatier Showers comic, my perception and principles on romance had dramatically shifted. The relationship dynamic between Tanz and Groover had always been a fan-favorite amongst my readers, however, through my personal growth and life lessons, that dynamic no longer represented my own approach towards relationships. At this point, using Tanz and Groover as a storytelling vehicle had become increasingly difficult. It wasn't until 2020 as the pandemic hit, while I was at the peak of my anxieties and depression, that I found clarity on how to repurpose Tanz and Groover's role to better reflect my world views. It became apparent to me then that the natural progression for Tanz and Groover would be to have them both explore new kinks together as a couple. In that respect, Preyford Dobermanners was created and retroactively added into the timeline (before their meeting with Pridestar) with the role of acting as a "kink guide" for both Tanz and Groover, and readers alike.

With all that said, bear in mind that what you see in the following pages isn't necessarily the only way to develop your comics. As a visually-oriented person, I begin my process primarily focused on these key things - the layout and composition of each page, the rhythm and pacing of the panels and visual flow of which the reader's eye travels across the pages while reading - which is why you'll notice the early drafts and thumbnails are mostly scribbles of boxes, panels and pages, with very rough suggestions of character drawings and placeholder images. Since I work visually, I very rarely ever have a script. Most of the writing at this stage are rough outlines and plot points that I want covered. Keeping things very rough and loose overall lets me easily reshuffle and edit things.

The 10th anniversary project probably began somewhere in 2019. At this point, it was still a very different comic altogether, with the timeline picking off where we left in the colored comics after the gang had their interactions with Pridestar. There was a bit of a time leap ahead, and the pup play scene was just a side arc in the larger story. Returning to my idea bank in 2020, I honed in on the pup play and changing room scene, extrapolating it into a proper standalone chapter. If you squint and look closely, significant chunks of the thumbnails made it into the final edit. A lot of the dialogue I write is done only towards the very end, most of which are improvised and rewritten many times to suit the pacing and size of the panels. My main criteria for my own character dialogues is that they have to be easy to read, snappy, and realistic enough to pass off as actual real-world conversation. Also, bonus points for being able to write with humor and slide in a punchline.

My process is about giving myself permission to experiment, make mistakes, learn the lessons needed to move forward and maintain an open mind to make the necessary edits and iterations to discover the best possible version of the story.

I hope this helps you find your own voice! Good luck!

Snares

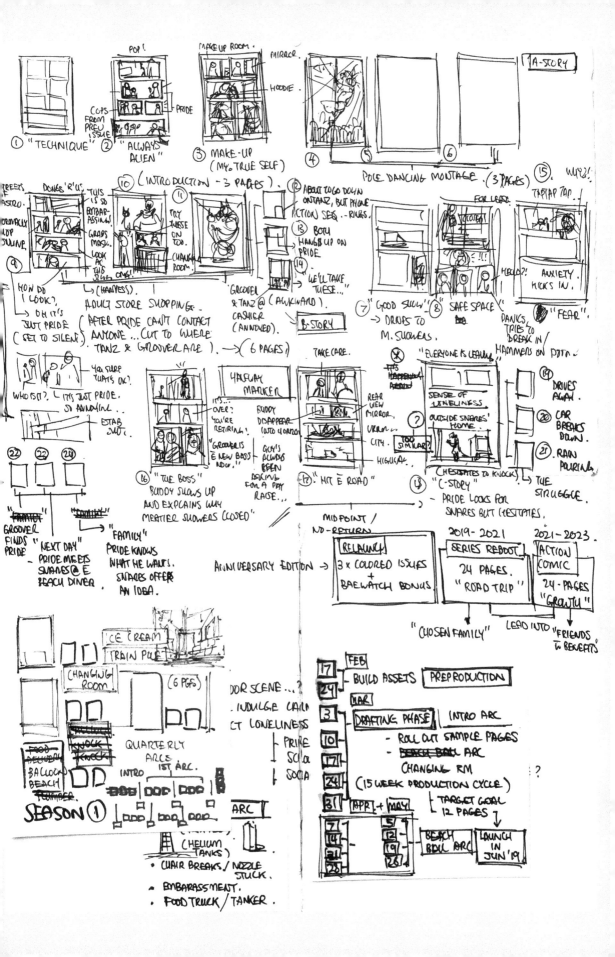

① "TECHNIQUE" ② "ALWAYS ALIEN" (99¢) — PRIDE / COPS FROM PREV ISSUE / POP!
③ MAKE-UP (MY TRUE SELF) — MAKE UP ROOM / MIRROR / HOODIE
④ ⑤ ⑥ | POLE DANCING MONTAGE. (3 PAGES) ⑮ WAX?! TAP TAP TAP.

| 1A-STORY |

⑨ HOW DO I LOOK? → OH IT'S JUST PRIDE (SET TO SILENT.)
STREETS / ASTRO / CAUTION UP SWING DONGS 'R' US
⑩ (INTRODUCTION - 3 PAGES) — THIS IS SO EMBARRASSING! GRABS MASK. LOOK AT THIS ONE!
⑪ TRY THESE ON TOO. CHANGING ROOM (HARNESS)
⑫ ABOUT TO GO DOWN ON TANZ, BUT PHONE ACTION SEQ. - RINGS.
⑬ BOTH HANDS UP ON PRIDE
⑭ WE'LL TAKE THESE... GROOVER & TANZ @ CASHIER (AWKWARD) (ANNOYED). | B-STORY |
⑦ "GOOD LUCK" → DRIVES TO M. SHOWERS. ⑧ SAFE SPACE HELLO?! ANXIETY KICKS IN. — FOR LEASE DANCE TRIES TO BREAK IN / HAMMERS ON DOOR ● "FEAR"

ADULT STORE SHOPPING. (AFTER PRIDE CAN'T CONTACT ANYONE... CUT TO WHERE TANZ & GROOVER ARE). → (6 PAGES)
YOU SURE THAT'S OK? WHO IS IT? → IT'S JUST PRIDE. SO ANNOYING. ESTAB SHOT
TAKE CARE. ⊗ IT'S HAPPENING AGAIN "EVERYONE IS LEAVING" SENSE OF LONELINESS OUTSIDE SNARES' HOME ⑦ HESITATES TO KNOCK → THE STRUGGLE ⑱ DRIVES AWAY.

HALFWAY MARKER IT'S... OVER? YOU'RE RETIRING! BUDDY DISAPPEAR INTO HORIZON REAR VIEW MIRROR / MIRROR CITY. / HIGHWAY TOO SIMILAR?

⑯ "THE BOSS" BUDDY SHOWS UP AND EXPLAINS WHY WEATHER SHOWERS CLOSED" "GROOVER IS THE NEW BOSS NOW." GUY'S ALWAYS BEEN ASKING FOR A PAY RAISE...
⑰ "HIT THE ROAD"
⑲ "C-STORY" - PRIDE LOOKS FOR SNARES BUT HESITATES.
⑳ CAR BREAKS DOWN. ㉑ RAIN POURING.

㉒ ㉒ ㉔ "FAMILY" GROOVER FINDS PRIDE "NEXT DAY" - PRIDE MEETS SNARES @ BEACH DINER "FAMILY" PRIDE KNOWS WHAT HE WANTS. SNARES OFFERS AN IDEA.
MIDPOINT / NO-RETURN

ANNIVERSARY EDITION → RELAUNCH 3 x COLORED ISSUES + BAEWATCH BONUS
2019-2021 SERIES REBOOT 24 PAGES "ROAD TRIP"
2021-2023 ACTION COMIC 24-PAGES "GRAVITY"
"CHOSEN FAMILY" LEAD INTO "FRIENDS W BENEFITS"

ICE CREAM / TRAIN PLATFORM / CHANGING ROOM (6 PGS)
..DOOR SCENE...? . INDULGE CARN.. CT LONELINESS → PRIDE / SCH.. / SOCIA..
FOOD DELIVERY / KNOCK KNOCK / BALLOON / BEACH / PLUMBER

QUARTERLY ARCS INTRO 1ST ARC.
SEASON ① | ODD | ODD | ODD | ARC I (HELIUM TANKS)
• CHAIR BREAKS / NOZZLE STUCK.
• EMBARRASSMENT.
• FOOD TRUCK / TANKER.

FEB 17 - BUILD ASSETS | PREPRODUCTION 24
MAR 3 | DRAFTING PHASE | INTRO ARC
- ROLL OUT SAMPLE PAGES
10 - BEACH BALL ARC CHANGING RM
17 24 (15 WEEK PRODUCTION CYCLE) ?
31 | APR + MAY ↳ TARGET GOAL 12 PAGES
7 5
14 12 BEACH BALL ARC LAUNCH IN JUN '19
21 19
28 26

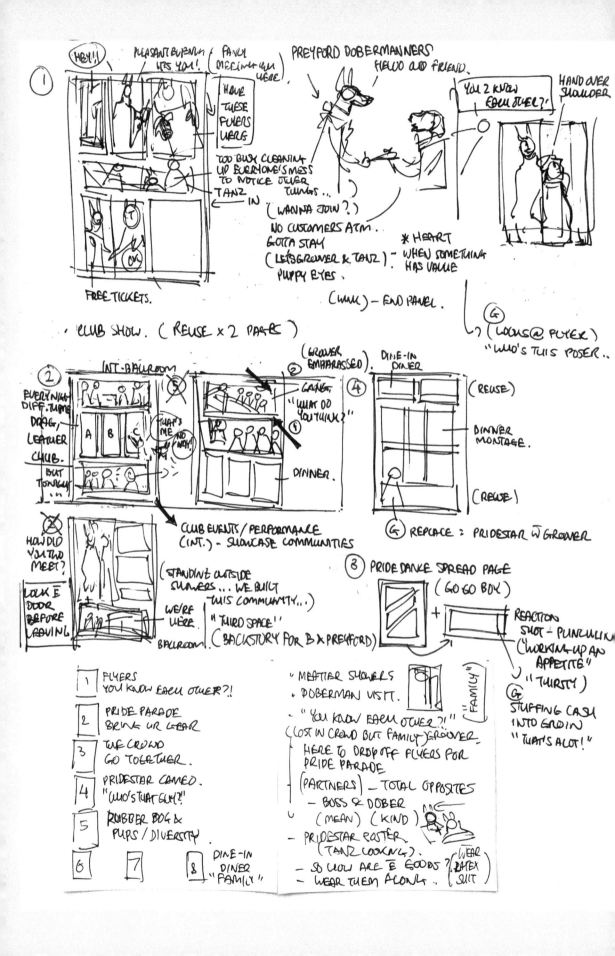

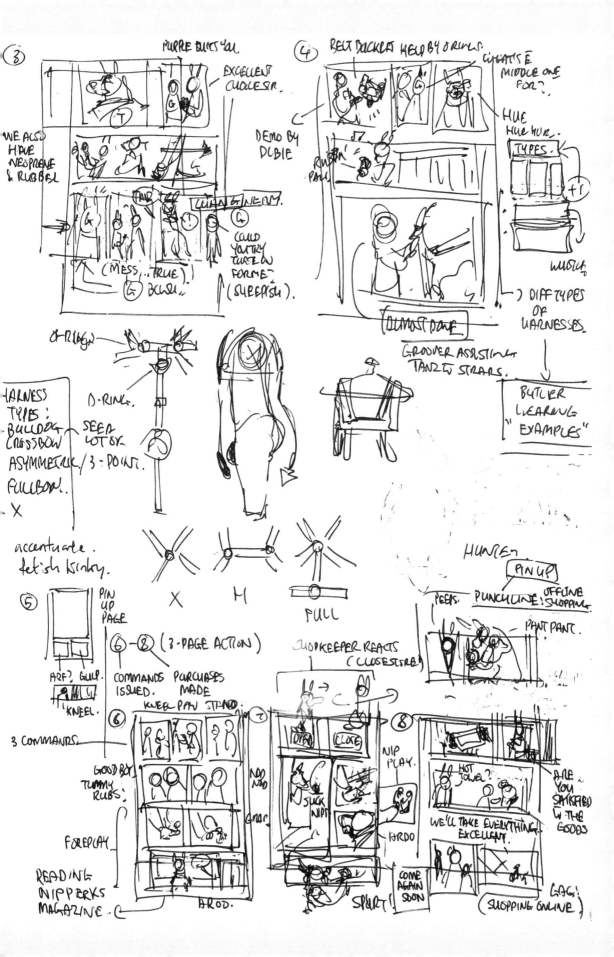

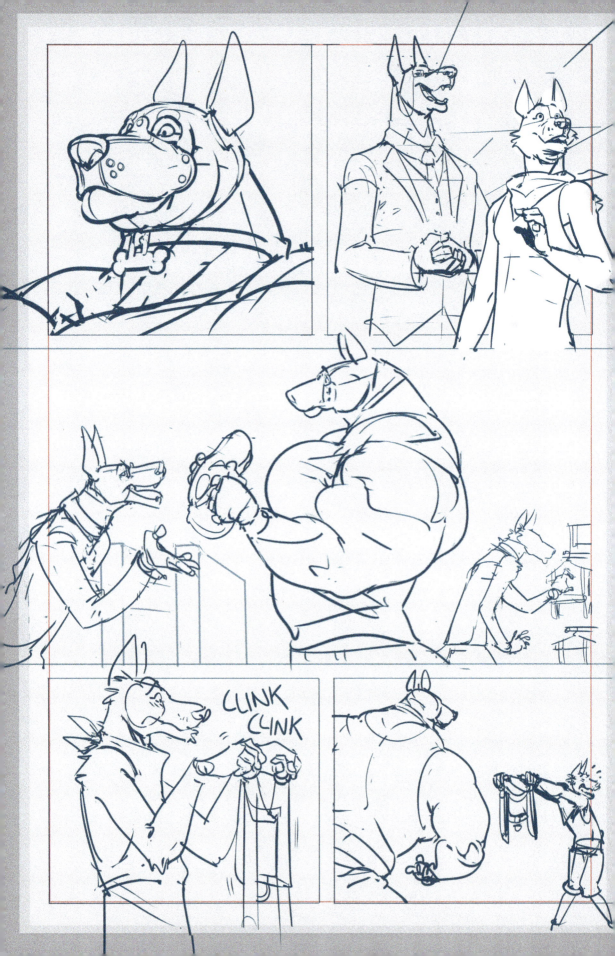

CHANGING ROOM

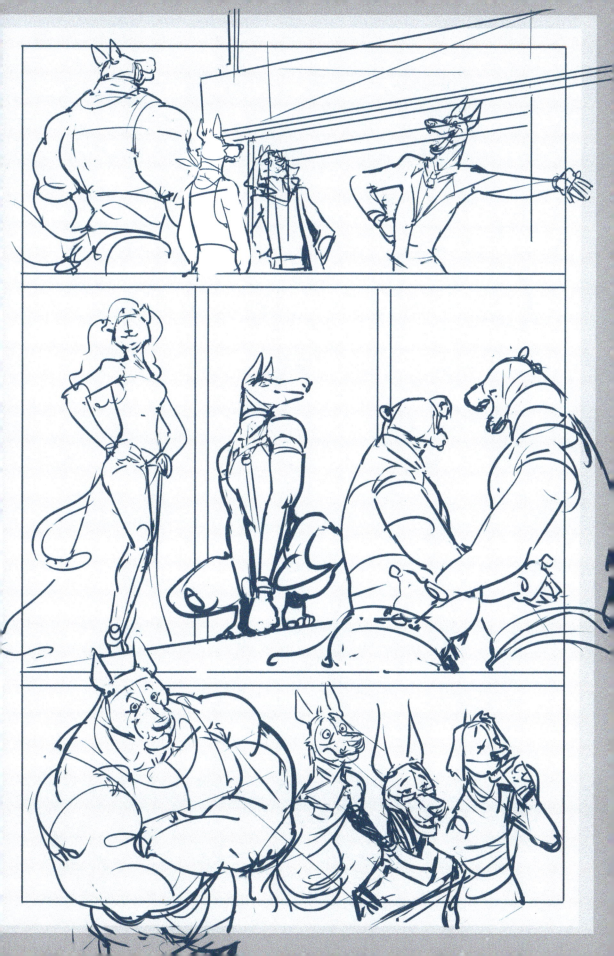

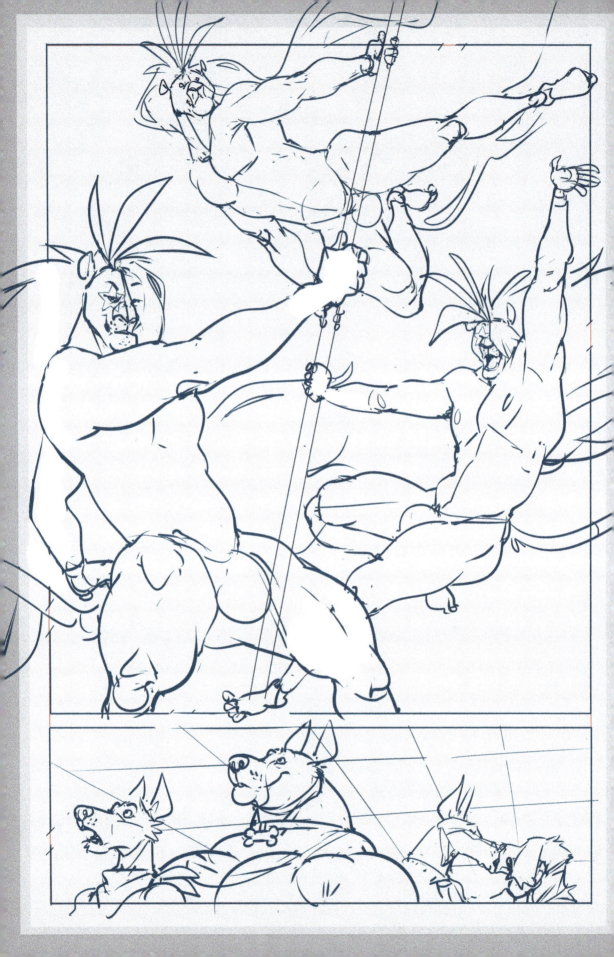

2020 - 2021 has been a very exhausting decade. I'm aware of what I've written. No, I'm not changing it. I'm right and you know it. As an artist who works primarily in the fandom it's been fascinating seeing the fandom continue without conventions. We rely on conventions not only for showing off fursuits, for profit, or buying stuff, but as an affirmation that the people we talk to online, who's work we see, and thoughts made public - come from people. In many ways, from people we care about.

Being flung into a very strange year - being approached to once again work on Meatier Showers has felt like a much needed return to normalcy with the promise of good things to come. I've always enjoyed working on these - I love Snares' writing and sense of visual storytelling. He's always had a fantastic capacity to point out something can be as sexy as it is absurd and not have those feelings be conflicting at all. A lot of the themes he explores in Meatier showers are about sex positivity. A theme I'll always stand behind.

I started as a fan of Snares. This developed into a friendship and a surprisingly excellent working relationship which being overseas and a pandemic couldn't wreck. So I can't think of a better love letter to Meatier Showers fans than another fun installment of a couple exploring new, fun, sexy, weird, fantastic things together, and in turn, making their relationship stronger. In many ways working with Snares was a return to normalcy that - that meant working with sweet thoughtful themes delivered through unconventional means.

What I learned during this last year (and while working on this) is the furry fandom is more committed to sticking together than we give ourselves credit for. And working on this comic, even during such turbulent times is evidence of that very thing.

Thanks for reading, and until next time!

Donryu

Printed in the USA
CPSIA information can be obtained
at www.ICGtesting.com
LVHW060744181223
766591LV00100B/4476